*Except for variations in time and character identification and placement, the events written in this story are true and actually happened.*

# GARY PAULSEN

# NIGHTJOHN

Published by
Bantam Doubleday Dell Books for Young Readers
a division of
Bantam Doubleday Dell Publishing Group, Inc.
1540 Broadway
New York, New York 10036

The trademark Laurel-Leaf Library® is registered in the U.S. Patent and Trademark Office.

The trademark Dell® is registered in the U.S. Patent and Trademark Office.

ISBN: 0-440-21936-1

RL: 4.6

Reprinted by arrangement with Delacorte Press

Printed in the United States of America

The text of this book is set in Bodoni Book

February 1995

OPM   33   32   31

*This book is dedicated to the memory of Sally Hemings, who was owned, raised, and subsequently used by Thomas Jefferson without benefit of ever drawing a single free breath.*

# NIGHTJOHN

# O N E

This is a story about Nightjohn. I guess in some ways it is a story about me just as much because I am in it and I know what happened and some of it happened to me but it still seems to be most about him.

Nightjohn.

There's some to say I brought him with witchin', brought Nightjohn because he came to be talking to me alone but it ain't so. I knew he was coming but it wasn't witchin', just listening.

It happened. How it came to be was that Nightjohn he came and it wasn't me, wasn't nobody one or the other brought him except maybe it was that God did it, made Nightjohn to come.

God and maybe old Clel Waller. He wants that we should call him "master," and they's some do when he can hear but we call him dog droppings and pig slop and worse things yet when he ain't listening nor close. He ain't no master of nobody except that he's got dogs and a whip and a gun and so can cause hurt to be on some, bad hurt, but he ain't no master for all of that. We just call him that when we have to. Keeps him from whipping on us.

I'm Sarny and they be thinking I'm dumb and maybe up to witchin' and got a stuck tongue because when I birthed they say I come out wrong, come out all backwards and twixt-and-twinst. But it ain't so that I'm dumb. I'm just quiet and they be thinking because I don't make noise and go to twattering all the time that I be dumb. But I ain't. I just be so quiet and listen all the time that I learn things.

I'm Sarny and the other part of my name be the same as old Waller who wants to be master but is nothing. Nothing. I don't count the back part of my name no more than I count old Waller himself. No more than I count spit.

My mammy she told me that my birthing mammy was sold when I was four years old because she was a good breeder and Waller he needed the money. My mammy said that my birthing mammy brought enough for four field hands and that she cried when the man bought her. My mammy say that my birthing mammy stood in the back of a wagon and watched back and waved and my mammy held me up so I could see the waving and hear her crying. But I don't remember that.

All I know for a mammy is the one that raised me, old Delie, and she be the one who raises all the young. Breeders don't get to keep their own babies because they be spending all their time raising babies and not working. So when they're born babies go to the wet nurse and she feeds them and then old Delie gets them and they don't live with their birthing mammies again even if they aren't sold off.

It isn't for certain how old I am except for the sticks. Mammy keeps a stick for each one of us and in the summer she cuts a notch on the stick for each of the girls so as to know when it will come time for the troubles and then the breeding. Waller puts great store in the sticks and watches them like a old hawk watching the chicken pens.

By the stick I am going into the same year as all the fingers on both hands, fold them down, then hold up the thumbs. Delie says it be twelve but I don't know numbers to count so that doesn't mean so much to me. I don't yet have the trouble so I am still left to be as a child. We work around the quarters and clean the yard and gather eggs and help mammy with the young ones. It's work, but it ain't dawn to dark hard work like the field work and it leaves me a bit of time to listen and see things. Mammy she tells me some things to learn and I hear some others from the field hands who come back at dark and now and again I have to work in the flower beds below the big window on the white house.

The house women are fond of leaving the window open and talking all their business right there. So when I'm in the flower bed below the window I hear more things to learn. When the day is coming on dark and we are all finished eating out of the trough in the front of the quarters I get onto the pallet in the back of the long log house with Delie and the babies and I lays there and thinks.

I thinks of all the things I have learned that day and then I tries to add them to the things I learned the day before and then the day before that. I've been doing that as long as I can remember, since I was almost just walking, and I remember all the parts of my life. If there is time of an evening and I haven't been worked to the bone I can just lay there in the dark and think on all my time and remember it. Except for my birthing mammy—I can't think on her at all except to wonder and wonder about her. Did she have dark skin or light? How was her voice, how did it sound? But you can't remember what isn't there and no amount of thinking on it will make it come into my brain.

It was in the flower bed that I first heard about Nightjohn. Not by name, but by happening.

# T W O

One morning I was below the window working in the roses. Some leaves had fallen because of the little green bugs that eat the roses and I had to chew tobacco leaves and spit on the plants to kill the bugs. I didn't much like to chew on tobacco leaves, though some of the men favored it, and it made me sick enough to near heave my guts. I had to stop and while I was stopped, just under the window down in the thick leaves and the soft dirt, I hears it.

"I swear—if Clel doesn't stop buying hands we won't have any money left for dresses." It was the missus talking to her sister. Her sister be an older woman never found a man, dried up and mean and she hates us. The missus is named Margaret and her sister named Alaine or something close to that. Course we never call them by their names. Never talk to them at all. And when we talk about them in the quarters and ain't nobody listening but quarters' people we call them same as the master. Call them dog droppings or horse crap.

"He went out and bought another hand," the missus said. "Over a thousand dollars. Honestly, he must think we're made of money."

I didn't know counting but I knew a little of money. Once I found a penny in the dirt by the quarters and I went to mammy and held it out.

"Hide that," she told me. "That's

money. Somebody see that and they'll come along and take it from you."

So I figured money was something to have and keep and I kept the penny, hid in the dirt at the end of the quarters and I still have it. Sometimes I take it out when there ain't anybody around and rub it on my shirtdress until it shines and shines.

And I knew that there was bigger money than a penny but I didn't know how that all worked, that bigger money, because it wasn't something I learned. So when the missus she said about a new hand costing a thousand dollars all I knew was that it was more than a penny. More than many pennies. Maybe more than all the pennies in the world because they be rich, the people in the white house.

Richer than God, mammy said once, but she was just mad and didn't mean it. She'd been praying and got caught at it. People in the quarters weren't supposed to pray nor know nothing about God. Mammy she prayed all the time, in her head. Usually she only prayed out loud late at night when there wasn't anybody to hear her. Sometimes she brought in the big cast iron kettle used for making morning food to pour in the trough for us to eat.

Mammy would put the kettle in the corner of the quarters, way back in the dark corner, and put her head inside the kettle so's the sound wouldn't carry and she'd pray in a whisper. She swore they could hear like cats up to the big house and the only way to keep safe was to pray in the kettle.

I one time put my head in the kettle with her.

"Lord Jesus," she said, talking to the bottom of the kettle. "Lord Jesus, you come be making us free. Free someday. In your name, amen."

I was small then and didn't know about being free, or even how to think about being free, or even what being free meant. So I asked her what free meant.

"Nothing to talk about now," she said. "You'll know when you get older but now you just be quiet and never, never say you heard me praying about being free."

Which I never did, even after I learned what freedom is and started praying for it my ownself. Even then.

The people in the white house aren't richer than God, I know that.

But they be rich, and they be spending a lot of money and they brought in the new hand for a thousand dollars.

And that be Nightjohn.

# T H R E E

Old Waller brought him in bad.

Sometimes they come in not so bad. Spec'lators bring them to sell sometimes all in a wagon, sell them from the wagon and Waller he buys them one or two or whatever, right from the wagon.

Sometimes Waller he goes for to buy them at some other place and brings them home in the wagon, sitting in the back. Old Waller on the seat with a pistol in his belt, sitting like he thinks he's big. Other places, near here, other places have what they call overseers to use the whip and to use the gun and go to get them. But not here. Waller he loves to carry the whip and carry the gun and so he rides in the wagon his ownself and makes on to be big. Sitting there like he don't know we hate him.

But he can bring them in good or he can bring them in bad and with Nightjohn he brought him in bad.

Not in the wagon. He was walking, all alone in front of the horse. Waller riding the big brown horse in back. Had a rope down and over to a shackle on Nightjohn's neck. Rope tied to the saddle. So when the horse stopped, Nightjohn he stopped, jerked on his neck.

Waller he brought Nightjohn into the main yard near the quarters out in the open, yelling and swearing at him. Yanking on the rope. Nightjohn he didn't have any clothes on, stood naked in the sun. I was by the quarters, carrying water to wash the eating trough before it was time for the evening feeding and I saw them.

Standing in the sun with the rope going from his neck up to the saddle, tired and sweating because Waller ran him. Dust all over him. Flies around his shoulders.

His back was all over scars from old whippings. The skin across his shoulders and down was raised in ripples, thick as my hand, up and down his back and onto his rear end and down his legs some.

I wondered why he was bought with all the marks. When they be marked that way people don't buy them because it means they hard to work, hard to get to work.

But he did. Waller he brought Nightjohn home and ran him naked till he sweated and the biting flies took at him and I was there and saw him come in.

I'm brown. Same as dark sassafras tea. But I had seen black people, true black. And Nightjohn was that way. Beautiful. So black he was like the marble stone by the front of the white house; so black it seemed I could see inside, down into him. See almost through him somehow.

In a little, Waller he untied the rope. Then he cracked the whip once or twice like he be a big man and drives Nightjohn past the quarters and out to the field to work. Didn't matter that he'd been run or might be thirsty. He didn't stop at the pump but ran him right on through and out to the fields, naked as he was born, to get to hoeing.

He come in bad and it wasn't until late that night, after dark in the quarters, that I learned his name.

Mammy she made canvas pants for

the new men when they came. Sewed them from the roll of tarp-cloth we used for all our clothes. She gave a pair to Nightjohn when they came in from the field but he didn't have time to say nothing because it was time for the evening food.

Two times a day at the wooden trough —that's how we eat. Mornings they pour buttermilk down the trough and we dip cornbread in it and sometimes pieces of pork fat. We take turns on a calabash gourd for a dipper to get all the milk out except the little ones don't always get much of a turn and have to lick the bottom of the trough when it's done. For midday meal the field hands —men and women both, 'less a woman is a breeder in her last month, then she can work the yard—each carry a piece of cornbread and pork fat or meat with them. When the sun is high overhead they stop long enough to stand and eat the bread and fat. They don't get to sit or rest. Even do they have to do their business they dig a hole with their hoe and do it standing and cover it with dirt and get back to work.

Don't they do this, don't they do it right, don't they keep standing and work even to eat and do their business, don't they do it all just exactly right the whip comes down on them. Old Waller he don't have overseers but they's two men he calls drivers. They have whips and clubs and use them.

Then at night, when it's just dark they come in from the fields. During the day mammy and the breeders that can still walk and the small ones that can't keep up to work in the fields yet make food.

We cook in the big pot mammy used for praying. We cook pork fat and vegetables from the garden and make skillet cornbread. When the field people come in at night we pour from the pot in the trough and everybody passes the gourd and eats with their hands and dips cornbread into the juice till it's gone. Then the young ones get to lick the trough and we go into the quarters for the night.

There ain't no light allowed in the quarters. Time was, mammy said, when she had a small bowl and made a lamp with a piece of cotton and melted pork fat but up to the white house they saw the light and made her put it out. Kept the workers awake, they said.

Course we be awake anyway, if we want to. Just be awake in the dark. Light comes through the open door and there are four small windows down the back wall. If there's a moon there be good light, light enough to see faces and talk and even if there isn't a moon enough comes from the stars and the lights from the white house to let us see a little.

Those to work in the field are always tired. Always caved in with work. And there ain't never enough to eat, so they be hungry, too. They usually go to sleep as soon as they hit the corn-shuck pallets on the floor.

But the first night when the new man was there you could tell it was going to be different. He didn't even get on the floor but went right over to the corner where mammy put the pot to pray sometimes and sat there. The new canvas pants were so stiff I could hear them crackle and bend when he sat back against the wall. I was on the side of mammy's shuck mattress along with about half a dozen young ones who were all kicking and scratching so sleep wasn't coming and I hear:

"Who's got tobacco? I need some tobacco."

It was a whisper, but loud, cutting from the corner where the new man sat. I had me some tobacco. It was just shredded bottom leaf that I'd been chewing to spit on the roses but I'd kept some back in a wrapped piece of sacking inside my shirtdress, tied round my waist on a piece of string. I didn't say a word. You come on things, things to keep, and you keep them to trade for other things. Things you need. Like pork fat. Or pennies.

He chuckled, low and rippling. Sounded like a low wind through willows, that small laugh, or maybe water moving over round rocks. Deep and soft.

"I'll trade," he whispered. "I'll trade something for a lip of tobacco."

I thought, What you got to trade? You come in naked as the day you was born, come in bad with whip marks all up and down your back, not even a set of clothes or canvas pants and you're ready to go to trading? I didn't say it, but I thought it. And he like to read my thoughts.

"What I got to trade, what I got to trade for a lip of tobacco is letters. I knows letters. I'll trade *A*, *B*, and *C* for a lip of chew." He laughed again.

And there I was, with the tobacco in my dress and he said that and I didn't know what letters was, nor what they meant, but I thought it might be something I wanted to know. To learn.

So mammy she was sleeping, her breath moving in and out, and I wiggled out of the pile of young ones and moved to the dark corner and set my ownself next to him. "What's a letter?"

He smiled. "You sound like you've got tobacco."

"Not until I know what a letter is. . . ."

"Why, it's reading. You learn the letters first and then when you know them you string them together into words. I'll trade you three letters for a lipful."

I knew about reading. It was something that the people in the white house did from paper. They could read words on paper. But we weren't allowed to be reading. We weren't allowed to understand or read nothing but once I saw some funny lines on the side of a feed sack. It said:

**100 lbs.**

I wrote them down in the dirt with a stick and mammy gave me a smack on the back of the head that like to drove me into the ground.

"Don't you take to that, take to writing," she said.

"I wasn't doing it. I was just copying something I saw on a feed sack."

"Don't. They catch you doing that and they'll think you're learning to read. You learn to read and they'll whip you till your skin hangs like torn rags. Or cut your thumb off. Stay away from writing and reading."

So I did. But I remembered how it had looked, the drawings on the sack and in the dirt, and it still puzzled me. I dug in my dress and found the tobacco but held it.

"You saying you can read?"

He nodded.

"I give you something to read, you can read it? Just like that?"

"I can."

There was some yellow light from the windows of the big house and it came through the doorway and made a light patch on the dirt floor.

"Come on."

I led him to the light patch and squatted. I used my finger to scratch what I remembered in the dirt. The floor was hard packed and I had to rub hard to make it show right.

"There."

He squatted and squinted.

"Why, those ain't letters. Those are numbers."

"Numbers?"

He nodded. "Sure is. Says one hundred. Then there's those three letters on the end. They don't work for me as a word. Just *L B S*—don't say a word. It must mean something to somebody."

"Can you teach me that?"

"To read?"

"To read what I just put there in the dirt—can you teach me?"

He rubbed his chin. "Well, mought be if I had some tobacco. . . ."

I dug the sack out of my shirtdress and gave him a pinch. He put it in the side of his mouth.

"Way it works," he said, "is you got to learn all the letters and numbers before you can learn to read. You got to learn the alphabet."

"Alphabet?"

He nodded. "There be lots of letters, and each one means something different. You got to learn each one."

"Those three you said back in the dark corner? Can you teach me those?"

"I sure can." He used the edge of his hand to rub out what I had written in the dirt. Then he made a drawing with his thumb.

## A

"Tonight we just do *A*." He sat back on his heels and pointed. "There it be."

I looked at it, wondered how it stood. "Where's the bottom to it?"

"There. It stands on two feet, just like you."

"What does it mean?"

"It means *A*—just like I said. It's the first letter in the alphabet. And when you see it you make a sound like this: *ayyy,* or *ahhhh."*

"That's reading? To make that sound?"

He nodded. "When you see that letter on paper or a sack or in the dirt you make one of those sounds. That's reading."

"Well that ain't hard at all."

He laughed. That same low roll. Made me think of thunder long ways off, moving in a summer sky. "There's more to it. Other letters. But that's it."

"Why they be cutting our thumbs off if we learn to read—if that's all it is?"

" 'Cause to know things, for us to know things, is bad for them. We get to wanting and when we get to wanting it's bad for them. They thinks we want what they got."

I thought of what they had. Fine clothes and food. I heard one of the house workers say they ate off plates and had forks and spoons and knives and wiped their mouths like they wiped their butts. "That's true—I want it."

"That's why they don't want us reading." He sighed. "I got to rest now. They run me ten miles in a day and worked me into the ground. I need some sleep."

He moved back to the corner and settled down and I curled up to mammy in amongst the young ones again.

*A*, I thought. *Ayyy, ahhhh.* There it is. I be reading.

"Hey there in the corner," I whispered.

"What?"

"What's your name?"

"I be John."

"I be Sarny."

"Go to sleep, Sarny."

But I didn't. I snuggled into mammy

and pulled a couple of the young ones
in for heat and kept my eyes open so I
wouldn't sleep and thought:

A.

# F O U R

Come a hard time then.

Come a awful, hard time.

There be a girl before then named Alice. She slept in the other end of the quarters and as soon as she got big she went to work in the fields picking and hoeing. But she was addled in the head, off dreaming sometimes, and mammy said one day that they would sell her. But her body was all right and they in the white house decided she be a good breeder so they set her for that.

She didn't take well to it and fought and they tied her to make it happen, in the breeding shed back of the quarters but it went bad on her head and her thinking. When it was done she was worse than before.

She wandered in the yard and sometimes even went up to the white house. Except for the house servants and gardening we weren't allowed to the white house and when the master one day caught Alice he took her to the wall of the spring house.

The spring house was where we got drinking water. It was made of stone and with heavy walls. They had rings of iron to be made in the walls many years past, big rings of iron with chains and shackles and they put Alice there and tore her clothes off.

Then the master he whipped her his ownself with a rawhide whip cut from an old gin belt used on the cotton gin.

Sometimes he doesn't whip and makes a field hand do it and stands with his pistol in his belt and smiles.

But sometimes he likes to take the whip and this time he whipped her until her back was all ripped and bleeding. We had to watch. Every time there was somebody to be on the wall of the spring house and be whipped or other punishments we all had to watch.

When it was done and she had screamed until she sounded like pigs being cut he made mammy to go to the salt house and get salt and rub it in the cuts to make more pain.

I never heard a sound like that. I'd seen men whipped but never that kind of sound, cutting like that, high and higher until it whistled in my ears.

Then he left her to hang there until the next day. The flies they came and mammy went out and covered her back with a cloth and kept some of them off so they wouldn't make maggots in the cuts.

Next morning they took her down and they was some maggot eggs but not so bad. I helped mammy clean Alice. We took her in the quarters and mammy she rubbed grease on Alice's back and I sat and held her hands because she kept trying to reach around and push mammy's hand away.

All the time she don't say anything. Not a thing. Not even the silly things she used to say and when we were done she lay on the floor in the corner like she was broken. Broken inside.

Mammy made her some root tea that smelled of bark but Alice wouldn't drink it. She just lay there all that night and the next three, four days. During that time John came and I talked to him about *A*, traded tobacco with him. For two nights he didn't do no work on the trade and went to sleep right after the trough because the master worked him so hard. On the third night after I traded for A—sometime that same night Alice ran.

My life is short, but some live long and the one thing we know, short or long—it's wrong to run. Not wrong because it's wrong. But wrong because nobody ever gets away.

I've seen two to try it. Both men. One was an old man named Jim who just couldn't take no more and one night he up and cut.

They set after him the next morning with dogs. Only the master, he don't only go his ownself but took five or six field hands with him to see so they can carry what they see back to tell us.

The dogs be mean. He feeds them things to make them mean. Blood things. Sometimes he'll take them to the fields and should a man or woman work a little behind the others, or behind the best man, who is whipped to speed—why, he sets the dogs on the slow one. And he don't pull them off right away, neither. Lets them go until they taste blood and want more of it.

They's mean, the dogs. They's big and red with tight hair and heads like hogs and mean as Waller his ownself. He keeps them in a stone pen by the side of the horse barn and they slobber and chew at the gate each time we walk by. Dirt mean.

Jim, he ran at night too but it didn't help. The field hands told us later. He cut and ran down to the river, ran in the water for a goodly distance, then on the top of a fence rail for as long as the fence ran and then dropped to the ground and just moved.

The dogs followed him all the way. The hands said that one dog even got up and ran on the top rail of the fence.

Only took half a day and they caught Jim.

The last bit, when he heard the dogs singing him, baying on him, Jim climbed a tree. Problem was, the tree wasn't higher than he could reach, nearly, and as high as he got, the bottom of him hung down where the dogs could reach him.

The master set the dogs on him and they tore and ripped what they could reach until there wasn't any meat on Jim's legs or bottom. The dogs ripped it all off, to hang in shreds. The field hands say he still didn't let go, nor never did. Even when he was dead his hands didn't let go and the master made the field hands leave him there. They's some wanted to take Jim down and bury him but he made them to leave him that way, hanging by his hands in the tree, for the birds to eat.

Second man was young. Name of

Pawley. He wasn't a big enough hand to be allowed to be a breeder in the quarters and so he went to looking. He snucked away and met a girl at a plantation down the road a piece and they sat in the moonlight with each other some nights. Pawley he made it back before wake-up time every night but one, the last one. He fell asleep in his girl's arms, fell asleep in the moonlight.

So they from the white house set out with the dogs and Pawley he didn't run, or try to get away. He was on his way home but they let the dogs to have him anyway, tear him up to bleed but not kill him. Then the master he tied him down and cut him like he did the cattle so he wouldn't run to girls no more, but the cut went wrong and Pawley he laid all night and bled to death without ever making a sound in the corner of the quarters.

So don't nobody run. Besides, I don't

think there's a place to run to. I heard talk once of some land, some land north but it's far away and it was only talk. Not something to know. Just something to hear. Like birds singing, the talk of the land north, or the wind in the trees.

But Alice cut and run that night.

She didn't get far. Down to the river and then sideways some. Her back was still ripped and sore and she must have moved slow. She might have kept moving all night but hadn't gone more than to the other end of the cotton fields—an easy small walk. Then she pulled herself under some brambles and was there when they found her.

He let the dogs to have her.

Didn't matter what she'd gone through, or that her thinking wasn't working right. The field hands with him told us he smiled his big white smile like the big white house, pale maggot white like his skin smile and let the dogs to have her. She didn't fight them or try to get away and they just tore at her. Tore at her until her whole front was torn and gone and she was bleeding from the chest.

She didn't die.

Alice be too tough for her ownself good. She didn't die and he made the hands to carry her back and put her in the quarters. Mammy sewed up what she could with canvas thread and greased and patched and she lived.

She be like Pawley. She didn't make sounds even while mammy was pulling at the torn flaps of skin and sewing them on her chest. Not a sound. Just stared and stared at the wall.

That night John called to me as he came past where I was trying to sleep.

"Tobacco girl—time for another letter."

I had been all day helping mammy and was tired and sad for Alice, how she be at the other end of the quarters, but I went just the same. I still had two letters coming for that first pinch of tobacco.

He was sitting on his heels in the open doorway.

I squatted next to him. "What's the next one?"

He used a stick with a sharpened end on it and wiggled in the dirt two half circles:

**B**

"*Bee,*" he said. "It be *B*."

"That sounds crazy. . . ."

"That's how you say the letter. *B*. It's for *behh* or *be* or *buh* or *boo*. That's how a *B* looks and how you make the sound."

I made it sound in my mouth, whispering. "So where's the bottom to it?"

"I swear—you always want to know the bottom to things. Here, here it is. It sits on itself this way, facing so the two round places push to the front."

Suddenly he's gone. One second he's there, the next he's slammed sideways and gone.

"What in the *hell* are you doing to her?"

Mammy was standing there, big and black and tall in the moonlight. "What you doing to this girl?"

She had come from the side and fetched John such a blow on his head that it knocked him back into the wall and on his back.

He come up quick and didn't cower none.

"Nothing. Not like you think. I'm teaching her to read."

"That's what I mean," mammy said. "What in the *hell* are you doing? Don't you know what they do to her if they find her trying to read? We already got one girl tore to pieces by the whip and the dogs. We don't need two."

I'd been quiet all this time, watching. Didn't seem so bad, what he was doing. Teaching me a few letters to know. Maybe a word or two. So I said it. "Doesn't seem so bad—"

*"Bad?"* Then she hissed like a snake. "Child, they'll cut your thumbs off if you learn to read. They'll whip you until your back looks knitted—until it looks like his back." She pointed to John, big old finger. "Is that how you got whipped?"

He shook his head. "I ran."

"And got caught."

"Not the first time."

She waited. I waited.

"First time I ran I got clean away. I went north, all the way. I was free."

I'd never heard such a thing. We couldn't even talk about being free. And here was a man said he had been free by running north. I thought, How can that be?

"You ran and got away?" mammy asked.

"I did."

"You ran until you were clean away?"

"I did."

"And you came *back*?"

"I did."

"Why?"

He sighed and it sounded like his voice, like his laugh. Low and way off thunder. It made me think he was going to promise something, the way thunder promises rain. "For this."

"What you mean—this?"

"To teach reading."

It's never quiet in the quarters. During the day the young ones run and scrabble and fight or cry and they's always a gaggle of them. At night everybody be sleeping. But not quiet. Alice, she's quiet. But they's some of them to cry. New workers who are just old enough to be working in the fields cry sometimes in their sleep. They hurt and their hands bleed and pain them from new blisters that break and break again. Old workers cry because they're old and getting to the end and have old pain. Same pain, young and old. Some snore. Others just breathe loud.

It's a long building and dark except for the light coming in the door and the small windows, but it's never quiet. Not even at night.

Now it seemed quiet. Mammy she looked down at John. Didn't say nothing for a long time. Just looked.

I had to think to hear the breathing, night sounds.

Finally mammy talks. Her voice is soft. "You came back to teach reading?"

John nodded. "That's half of it."

"What's the other half?"

"Writing." He smiled. "Course, I

wasn't going to get caught. I had in mind moving, moving around. Teaching a little here, a little there. Going to do hidey-schools. But I got slow and they got fast and some crackers caught me in the woods. They were hunting bear, but the dogs came on me instead and I took to a tree and they got me."

Another long quiet. Way off, down by the river, I heard the sound of a night-bird. Singing for day. Soon the sun would come.

"Why does it matter?" Mammy leaned against the wall. She had one hand on the logs, one on her cheek. Tired. "Why do that to these young ones? To Sarny here. If they learn to read—"

"And write."

"And write, it's just grief for them. Longtime grief. They find what they don't have, can't have. It ain't good to know that. It eats at you then—to know it and not have it."

"They have to be able to write," John said. Voice pushing. He stood and reached out one hand with long fingers and touched mammy on the forehead. It was almost like he be kissing her with his fingers. Soft. Touch like black cotton in the dark. "They have to read and write. We all have to read and write so we can write about this—what they doing to us. It has to be written."

Mammy she turned and went back to her mat on the floor. Moving quiet, not looking back. She settled next to the young ones and John he turned to me and he say:

"Next is *C*."

Come more hard times.

A week goes by, then another week. It's the time of year for planting and the field hands have to work until they drop. Waller whips them past that and they get so tired they don't know up from down.

But John works with me. Not each night, because he's too tired. Some of them to work in the fields can't even walk back. Have to be carried by others. But some nights he works with me.

I learn a whole family of letters. All the fingers on one hand, two on the other. *A, B, C, D, E, F,* and *G.* He makes me to write them in the dirt and shows me how to take more than one of them and make a word, how the word is to be looking and how the word is to be sounding.

"Make it slow, make the sound each time. First the letter, then the sound, then make it to meet the sound from the next letter. Write *B,* say it, then *A* and say it, then *G. Bag.*"

And I make the word. First word.

*Bag.*

I make the word. I couldn't believe it. I came to make the word. Don't matter what the word is, what it means. Just to make the word. The first word.

That's what caused the trouble. Me and that first word.

I was so excited to be making a word I went everywhere and made the word. I took a stick and rubbed a point on it against a stone and round in back of the quarters I made the word in the dirt.

Wrote *BAG*. Then said it. *"Bag."*

I rubbed it out with my heel and wrote it in a new place. *BAG*. Wrote it all over. *BAG. BAG. BAG.* Each time I rubbed it out and moved to a new place and I was just looking at it, last time I wrote it, wondering if I could use other letters to make other words, thinking how to make another word when I hear the bull voice of Waller.

"What are you doing?"

A big hand grabbed the back of my shirtdress and dragged me up off my feet so I be hanging there.

"Tell me what you're doing." He was ugly. Pale white maggot ugly and I could smell his ugliness on him—white ugly. Stink of bad sweat and whiskey and smoke and fat food. I didn't say nothing.

He shook me like a dog shaking a rat. I felt my eyes go to wobbling and I just about messed. I still didn't say a word.

"What are you scribbling in the dirt?"

I thought, I'll lie. "Nothing. Something I saw on a old feed sack. I didn't know it was wrong to make it in the dirt."

"It looks like writing to me." Holds me up. Closer. Stink of his breath in my face. White stink. Pig stink.

"Don't know nothing about writing."

He hit me then. Be holding me with both hands, one on each shoulder so I'm facing him, and he quick drops one hand and hits me with his fist alongside the head as I fall.

I saw lights. Exploding colors.

"Don't lie to me. You tell me the truth of it and I'll let you off. Where did you learn to write?"

"Don't know nothing about writing," I said again. I had dropped all the way down and I was sitting in the dirt looking up at him but it put me in a bad place. Near his feet. Big boots. Black boots but wrong kind of black. Bad black, not good black like John. Mammy. Me. My mind rolled around like a sick dog.

He kicked me in the stomach.

"God damn you—don't you lie to me. I'll tie you to the spring house and get the truth out of you."

"Don't know nothing about writing. . . ."

He kicked again but he missed. First time I had grabbed my stomach, rolled away, and on the second kick I crawled-ran to get away. Ran to the only place I knew. Ran to the quarters. Ran to mammy.

She be in the corner changing the grease and rag on Alice's back and I ran to her dress and hid my head in the folds.

"What . . . ?" She held my arm. "What are you doing?"

"Hiding from him."

"Who?"

"Waller."

But Waller, he owned it all. Wasn't no safe place. He owned all the land, owned the quarters. Owned mammy. He came into the quarters then and saw me and took me by the arm. He held me, but he looked at mammy.

"Who is teaching her to read?"

"Sir?" Mammy gave him the big-eyed look. Look like she don't know nothing since she be born.

Waller he stood, looking at her. Breathing. Breath cut in, cut out like a saw cutting wood. I thought of the word, making the word. *Bag.* How making the word can cause all this and I hated my-self.

"All right," Waller said. "If that's the way you want it."

And he grabbed. Not me. I made the word but he didn't grab me. He grabbed mammy by the wrist and dragged her out of the quarters and across the dirt to the spring house and shackled her in the chain and bracelets on the wall.

Then he left her there, hanging, and went to the house. I had followed them across to the spring house and when he was gone I went up to mammy.

"He's going to whip you," I said. I was crying.

She sighed. Soft sound. And she looked up at the sun and the trees by the white house. "Birds sure do sing nice, don't they? They make the prettiest sound."

"It's all my doings." I pulled at the chains but they don't give. "I be making the word and forgot where I was and he saw me and now he's going to whip you."

Her eyes came on me then. I was crying but she wasn't. Her eyes came on me and they were sharp and her mouth was tight. "He would have whipped me anyway someday. Some other reason would have come along. He loves to use the whip."

"John." I thought of him. "John will stop him."

She shook her head. "He can't. No matter what he says, it won't stop Waller from whipping me. Now you go along and bring me some water when they ain't watching. He won't whip me until close on dark when everybody's back from the field to watch. The sun is hot and I'll be getting a big thirst, don't I get some water."

I snucked mammy water through the afternoon and she hung there. Way the chains and bracelets were, she couldn't reach down to sit so she had to stand. But standing through the day that way without moving is hard. After it passed some long time her legs didn't do so good and she sagged, and come late in the day she was 'most hanging on the chains. Her arms were up and she was having to hurt. I stood and watched for a spell and cried some but she stopped me.

"You take care of the young ones. Go now. They'll be dirty and stinking, if you don't change the rags on them. You run along. I be fine."

Took forever, waiting on the day. Mammy hanging that way. I thought once of running to the fields to tell John. Wouldn't do no good. Driver working the fields, he see me coming he just put me to work. They say if you can walk to the fields you can work. So I be working and not here and John couldn't do nothing anyway. They just keep him there no matter what I say.

So nothing.

Waller he keep his white maggot ownself in the white house all the day. Don't come out but once to see me standing by mammy. The sun works across the sky, cooking her. I brought her water again and a piece of cornbread I'd been saving since morning food but she shook her head.

"I'll just throw it up when he comes to whipping me. You go now—get the rags ready for my back and the salt."

"I can't."

"Yes. You can. Go do it."

Finally it came on to be dark and the hands come in from the field. Part of the afternoon I had the young ones to make a trough of cold food so they had enough to eat. They had to walk past the spring house and they saw mammy but there wasn't nothing they could do.

I went up to John and told him what had happened.

"Damn." He shook his head. "I should have warned you about making words."

"I knew. I was just excited. To be making my first word. I got to writing it in the dirt and he caught me. Waller caught me. He's going to whip her. Mammy. Going to whip her into rags."

John didn't say anything. He looked to where mammy hung on the spring house. His eyes were flat. "Bastard."

I was going to say more, say can you stop it, can you say something, but I heard the door on the white house open and Waller came out. He made gas and spit like he'd just ate a big meal and walked across the yard. Stopped.

"All of you get out here and watch." He bellered like an old bull, then turned. Didn't go to the spring house. Didn't have a whip.

Instead he went to the barn and went inside.

Come out in a breath or two and he was carrying a horse harness.

He went to the buggy by the carriage shed and hooked the harness like he had a horse in it, except it was empty.

Then he went back to the spring house. Looked at mammy.

"You going to tell me who's teaching them to read?"

Mammy been hanging but she stood now and gave him the big eye again. "I don't know nothing about reading or writing."

"God damn you."

He hit her with his fist. Then he unhooked her from the chains and ripped her clothes from off her body and dragged her naked to the harness.

"Put it on—I feel like a ride in the buggy."

Mammy put the collar around her neck with the lines going back to the buggy. Stood there. Looking up at the sky. I couldn't keep my eyes down. But the men did, they didn't look at her. Looked at the ground.

Waller climbed into the buggy and sat in the seat. He reached under the footboard and come up with a whip.

"Pull, damn you."

The whip snaked out from the buggy seat like it was alive and flicked and blood come on mammy's shoulder. Big cut. She started pulling but it wasn't good enough. She strained and heaved and the wagon it moved and Waller kept saying:

"Faster, damn it, faster."

And the whip come again and again, blood running down her back, the buggy moving across the yard and I hear in back of me:

"She don't know nothing. It was me that taught the girl the letters."

I turned and John was standing there. He had stepped forward and he pointed to mammy.

"Let her be. She don't know nothing about it. It was all me."

Waller looked at him the way a cat looks at a mouse caught in a corner. He smiled. Ugly smile.

"Well—I might have guessed." He stepped down from the buggy and moved to John. "Why don't you just go over there and put yourself in those irons on the spring house wall?"

I thought John wasn't going to do it. He held for one, two blinks of my eyes. Waller had the whip in his left hand, coiled but ready. His right hand was on the butt of the big pistol in his belt.

Two blinks, then John moved. He walked to the spring house and put the bracelets on. He wasn't wearing a shirt and when he turned his back the sun caught the scars from the old whippings. Rippled and ridged.

There's nowhere for the whip to hit, I thought. Can't hit nothing new. No new meat. Stupid. The way my thinking worked.

But Waller, he wasn't set for whipping.

He made one of the field hands to fetch the stump used for chopping the heads off chickens. Sent another hand to the blacksmith lean-to for a wide chisel and a hammer.

Then he turned to us. All standing, watching. I had moved to mammy but she shook her head. Stood.

"It is wrong to learn to read." Waller's voice loud, bouncing off the buildings. "It is against the *law* for you to read. To know any letters. To know any counting is *wrong*. Punishment, according to the *law*, is removal of an extremity."

We don't know all the words. Never heard "extremity" before. But we don't need to know.

Waller had two field hands to hold one of John's feet on the block. He put the chisel to the middle toe and swung the hammer.

*Thunk.*

The toe came off clean, jumped away from the chisel and fell in the dirt. Blood squirting out, all over the block. John he jerked the foot so hard it knocked one of the field hands over. But quiet, not even a grunt out of him. He didn't look down either. Just kept staring off into the fields next to the spring house.

"Other foot." Waller spit and wiped the chisel off on the stump.

The two field hands grabbed John's

left leg. The one next to the wall of the spring house—his name is Robe—he take it slow. Doesn't move fast so you could see it was bothering him and Waller snaps like a breaking stick.

"It can be your toe, too. It doesn't cost more to cut another one off."

So Robe he puts John's foot up there and Waller puts the chisel on it.

*Thunk.*

This time was not so clean. The foot jerks back and the toe is caught by some skin the chisel missed.

"Hold it up, damn it."

They hold the foot to the block. John he still not making any sounds, but his face is stiff. Like it's carved out of rock. And there's sweat pouring off his forehead, his neck, down his chest. He's soaked.

Waller cuts the last bit of skin.

"There. That'll teach you to mess

with things you shouldn't. Get a rag and some grease on that."

He walked back to the white house without looking back and as soon as he was away from us we went to helping.

The two hands carried John between them to the quarters and I went to mammy.

"Fetch the salt," she told me. "Get it in these cuts and 'fore I pass out for God's sake cover me with something so I ain't naked before the Lord."

So I did. And she swooned some with the pain and went down. And I frotched her dress and helped to put it on her and then helped her back to the quarters because her legs they didn't work right from hanging and standing all day.

All the time I'm thinking, be a hell, be a good hell with fire and brimstone and devils cutting skin off backs like mammy says. Be a good goddamn hell with demons eating at you, pulling your guts out—be the worst hell there is to be.

And put Waller in it.

John he down for three nights.

Mammy come up right away, but we grease and wrapped John's feet in rags mammy boiled in the pot for cooking food and he stayed on his back.

For the first night he was quiet and didn't say nothing. Just to lay and look at the ceiling, night and day, except to use a can mammy put there for him to use.

Second night he call me over to where he lay.

"What?" I ask.

"*H*."

"What?"

"That's the next letter. *H*. It sounds *huhh*, or *hehh*. It's a funny letter because it doesn't make any difference how it stands. Goes up, goes down, doesn't matter. It's the same."

He makes the letter in the dirt.

## H

Mammy she was in the other end and she came walking down to us. The young ones be out playing. Everybody else in the field. I thought she would roar at him, maybe gut him.

But she's smiling.

"Are you addled in the brain?" she asked.

He nodded. On his side, laying like a broke dog. He smiled back. "I don't get smarter. Just older."

"You know what he'll do if he catches

you teaching letters again? You ain't got so many more toes."

"Two more nights, I'm gone."

"On those feet?"

"On these feet."

"You'll bleed out. I knew you were going, but wait a week."

"How did you know I was going?"

"You were always going. When you came here they brought you in the collar. You are born to leave."

John's smile grew wider. "We should have met some other place."

"And other time." Mammy she snorted. "I make two of you, old enough to be your mother."

John laughed. Rolling deep sound. "Maybe so that doesn't matter so much. . . ."

Mammy she went on and he lay back. Looked to me. "Make the *H*. Make the sound, then the letter. When you get done, fetch me a piece of rawhide from the barn, so big." He held up his hands. "I need to make some shoes."

And in two nights, like he said, he was gone. He made the shoes out of rawhide and put rags around his toes and on the night he was to leave he made me to frotch him lard and pepper.

"For the dogs," he said. He rubbed the lard thick on the bottom of each shoe and wiped pepper in the lard and stood to leave. "Throws their smell off to the side."

Everybody asleep. Even mammy. Except me.

"I'll be back," he said. "Got some things to do and I'll be back."

But I knew he was lying. Just being good, saying the good things to hear. He ain't coming back, I thought, and watched him leave, hobbling on his stiff shoes and sore feet covered with rags.

Man gets out of here, I thought, gets clear again, he won't never come be here again. Never coming back.

Not unless the dogs catched him.

## SEVEN

Wrong again.

Only not right away.

He made it clean away. The next day Waller he took the dogs and two field hands and his horse and set off swearing and stinking. Two days he be gone, and he come back and make a storm around the place so we all know John he made it. He be gone.

Mammy she cried in a happy way and I smiled some for a time and hoped him well, though he left me hanging. I had only the same letters as on both hands. *A, B, C, D, E, F, G, H, I, J.*

I could write them and read them and I took to making words in my head with them. Made *HID*. And *FIB*. And *JAB*. And *HAD*. And *BIG*.

Other words. But I didn't dare write them in the dirt. Waller catch me and he'd make a tobacco pouch out of my skin. So I did them in my head, and tried to see the words, see the letters. But summer went, and then we took in crops. Cotton and corn and killing pigs came. Into fall. I still tried to make the letters in my head, and the words.

But my troubles came and though I hid it I knew they'd get to finding out and send me to the breeding shed.

I was in a misery. Mammy she worked to cheer me but it didn't do any good. I was feared and worried day to day that I'd be found out.

Come a night in winter. Leaves gone,

pigs all killed and hams hanging in the smokehouse. I sat in the dark, in the corner of the quarters, wishing I could go back a season to where I didn't have the troubles, and I heard a sound next to me in the dark and it was him.

John.

Be right there, next to me.

"Come on," he said.

"What?"

"Follow me. We got to go so's you can get back before first light."

"Go where?"

He smiled. Took my hand. Led me to the door. "School—we got to go to school. Don't you want to learn the rest of the letters?"

"But—"

And we go.

I was never off the place. Been only once to the fields where the corn and cotton grow. John he take me across the fields, out the other end into thick trees, down into some brushy ditches along the river.

Suddenly he stopped.

It be pitch dark. Any light from the stars can't get through the trees and brush and we stand for two, three deep breaths.

Then I smell it. Smoke. Faint smoke and John he leads me down a ditch until we hit a wall of solid brush. The smoke smell is strong now, stink of pitch burning. John he whistle like a catbird and there was a rustle of brush and then a slit of yellow light opened and he pulled me into the brush.

Inside the brush.

There is light, bright yellow from three pitch torches being held by three people. But there's more people there. Same as all on one hand, thumb and the one next to it on the other.

They're all smiling at me. I don't

know any of them but they're all smiling. Short boy comes up to me.

"We're from over the hill at the Stankin place. Two from there and the rest from Placers."

I didn't know nothing about those places but I smiled back. "You all know John from before?"

He nodded. "He come at night. Tell us to learn some letters, then tell us to come here. To school."

I didn't know what a school was, what it was supposed to be. This was slats of brush dragged and pushed over a ditch, thicker and thicker and closed in on the ends.

Be a pit.

Pit school.

John he moved to the end and held one of the torches up. In the other hand he held a book. I'd seen a book. Saw one of the women at the white house looking into one.

"This is a catalog." John held the book up. "It is full of things you can send for and own if you have money. They use it all the time. The whites. You read it, and it will tell you things. It has pictures and writing to talk about the pictures. Each of you come up and see it. Be quick now. We only have a couple of hours and I want to give you some letters. Sarny, you know some of them. You help me."

Everybody look at me.

"Only know this many," I said, holding up my hands.

"That's a good start. They don't know more than one or two. So you help me until we get to how many you know. Then we can all work together."

We look at the catalog and I can't believe it. Here in the school, pit school covered over so the light won't show out of the ditch from the torches, we look at the catalog. All the things we don't have. Dresses and shoes with buttons and little gloves and pretty hats and overalls and I started crying. Thinking of all the things, all the pretty things, and then I see it.

Picture of a horse. Got a thing around his head for feeding him, around his head and hanging over his nose.

*BAG.*

Says it right there. Under the picture. There's other words, but right there it says to me: *BAG.*

"I know this one." I pointed out the word, the word to John. "This one right here. It is *bag.* That's a bag on a horse's nose."

He laughed. Love the laugh. Same deep black laugh. Like night thunder. "Soon, Sarny, soon you'll be able to read them all. All of you will. Now let's start so you can get back."

And we do.

I take a stick, rub some dirt clear and

draw the lines in the dirt for three of
them who watch.

## A

Feels good to write again.

# WORDS

Late he come walking.

Late in the night when they in the white house are all asleep and we be asleep and nobody can know nothing, late when the moon is down and the stars are hiding in clouds, late when it isn't the day before and it don't seem like ever the new day will come—that late he come walking.

In the night he come walking. Late in the night and when he walks he leaves the tracks that we find in the soft dirt down by where the drive meets the road, in the soft warm dirt in the sun we see his tracks with the middle toe missing on the left foot and the middle toe missing on the right and we know.

We know.

It be Nightjohn.

Late he come walking and nobody else knows, nobody from the big house or the other big houses know but we do.

We know.

Late he come walking and it be Nightjohn and he bringing us the way to know.

# Turn the page for a preview of the long-awaited companion novel to the bestselling <u>Nightjohn</u>.

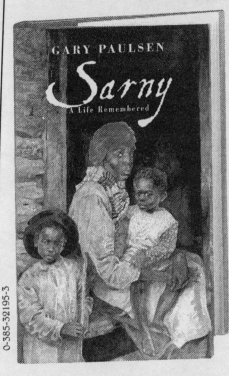

So many readers have written and asked: What happened to Sarny, the young slave girl who learned to read in *Nightjohn?* This riveting saga by master story-teller Gary Paulsen follows Sarny from her first moments of freedom at the end of the Civil War until her last days in the 1930s, and gives readers a panoramic view of America in a time of trial, tragedy, and hoped-for change.

0-385-32195-3

BFYR 154

Excerpt from *Sarny* by Gary Paulsen

Copyright ©1997 by Gary Paulsen

Published by Delacorte Press, Bantam Doubleday Dell Publishing Group, Inc., 1540 Broadway, New York, New York 10036.

# THREE

I had never seen the town. Had heard of it, talk all the time of all the houses and people and stores. Some of the men went now and again to help load and they came back with stories of men in frock coats and women in long dresses and carriages so fancy it seemed you could eat them. Billy he said he saw a black man eating hard candy from a sack. I had never even seen hard candy let alone eat of it and he said they had it in the stores and would sell it from jars a penny a bag but Billy now and again saw hants and heard whispers others didn't hear so I didn't believe everything he went on about.

The ax-faced man with the wagon had come from the road to town and had taken my children down that road and that's the way I went. Couldn't help but nearly run. They'd been gone six—no, seven—days and maybe they were in that town and I could find them there and my feet they just wouldn't walk slow.

Still I hadn't walk-trotted a mile when Lucy she caught up with me. Tall girl, leggy so she could move, sixteen, seventeen years old with a smile all the time even when things weren't funny. Sometimes she made me think of myself when I was younger though maybe she was a bit smarter and a good bit prettier. Didn't show the smart but it was there.

"Decided to come with you. That's what I *wanted* to do," she said when she caught up. "Except I didn't know you'd be running. It like to killed me catching up."

"They took my children," I said. "I can't walk slow—"

"I know. I was there. Don't you worry, we'll find little Delie and Tyler. Don't you worry." And there was that smile. "Waller he was still laying there when I left."

"I don't care a snip about Waller."

"It's good he's dead."

"I don't care."

"Maybe the pigs will eat him."

I didn't say anything more about him and never did say another word on him until I was old and even now could I see him, Bible or no, I wouldn't forgive him. Spit on his grave.

I didn't know how far it was to town but Lucy had heard it from Billy. "Seven miles," she said. "A mile is the same distance as the length of that south cotton field. So it would be seven of those fields. I figure we've walked three fields so there be four more. To town.''

She was carrying a sack that was heavier than mine, big weight down in the bottom. "What's in the sack?"

Her smile widened, seemed to cover her whole face. "Got me an extra shift in there.''

"Heavy shift."

"I stopped by the smokehouse on my way out and took two hams. They ain't big but they looked done and I figured we earned them.''

"We earned everything—''

"Riders.'' There was the sound of hooves.

Hard word. Riders. Them that run and come back talk about riders. Men on horses. Hard men. Mean to the bone men with guns and whips and chains and dogs. Riders is the word for the hard men.

But it's wrong this time. These riders are wearing blue, brass buttons glinting in the sun, rattle of sabers and creak of saddles. There were twelve of them, two by twos with a man in charge, an officer, out to the side and a little ahead.

We moved off the road to let them by but they stopped. Officer first, then all the men, stopped and looked down on us.

"You're free now." The officer brushed at a fly that had been following the horses and buzzed his face.

"I know. Yes sir. Thank you. The soldier at the plantation told us that—"

"But there are still dangers. We are just an advanced unit. There are bands of renegade scavengers—rebel deserters—that we haven't rounded up yet, killing and looting."

New word. Scavenger. Didn't know it. But knew the others—killing, looting. "Yes sir."

"You might want to find a safe place to be until things settle down. Look for some Union troops encamped and stay close to them."

"I can't. I've got children to find."

He had been looking away and he looked down on me now. Tall horse, tall man, looked down and smiled like he was a father. "Stay away from people on the roads unless they are soldiers."

"Yes sir."

And they were gone, the horses trotting past. Some of them looked at Lucy and some looked at me and their looks weren't as soft as the officer's. Looking at our shifts, way we stood. Two looked back as they rode away and I thought the officer was right, might be dangerous along the road especially at night. And from more than scavengers. But I didn't say anything and when I turned I saw Lucy and she was smiling back at the men and I thought, too much tooth in *that* smile. Might as well light a lantern and hang it over the store.

"Let's go."

It was afternoon, hot and muggy, and I kept moving and had there been time it would have been a marvel to see the country we traveled through.

Must have been a plantation every mile. Some of them nicer than the one I'd lived on and most of them less and all of them in smoke. Some big houses burning, some barns, sheds. Quarters burning all over the place. Blue-coated soldiers were everywhere. Moving this way and that. All seemed to have a reason to move, a place to get to, a place to leave. A lot of busy work.

Didn't see any gray soldiers except dead ones. Saw a group in a ditch, almost in a row, must have fallen like they stood. All their coats were open to show their bellies and some of them had big holes, some weren't marked so you could see it but they were all dead. Didn't see any dead blue ones, only gray.

Lucy she made the hex sign when we passed the bodies, little and first finger out and thumb down but I shook my head. "They won't bother you. Not now."

"They got spirits," she said. "They all got spirits can come back and hant us."

I didn't think so. They just looked like busted dolls to me but I didn't say anything more about it. Lucy she wanted to make the hex sign it didn't hurt anything and maybe it would help.

Black folks around every corner, over every rise. Some walked with the blue soldiers, following them, smiling but scared-looking like they thought it wouldn't last. Like you could be free and then not free. Not me, I thought, you try to turn me back into a slave and you've got your hands full. Might as well try to turn sawdust back into a tree.

Others they just looked dazed. Didn't know where to go, how to get there. Some followed us for a spell and I looked back once to see six or seven trotting behind us but we set too pushy a pace and they all fell away.

Every one I see, every single one I asked about little Delie and Tyler. Every soldier and every black person and they all try, think hard and try, but none remember seeing them, not even the wagon and the ax-faced man.

Town wasn't like they said. We came to the edge of it in the evening, just as the light was changing and it was getting hard to see. Part of it was light but most of it was smoke. Some buildings were all burned down, some were still burning. I didn't see any fancy carriages or hard candy or pretty dresses or frock coats.

Nothing but ruin. There were no men, no black men, no white men. Some women were there, white women except with all the soot on them they looked black and I stopped one of them on the outskirts. Woman maybe forty, looked sixty, seventy, kept picking at her dress.

"Could you tell me where they take slave children?" I asked. "To sell them?"

But she didn't answer, just looked past me, past Lucy at where a building used to be and there wasn't anything but burned boards and smoke. "We had a store there. We had a store right there. See? Right there where—"

"I had two children, miss," I said. "They came here on a wagon. They must have come here. They were this high, to my waist and a bit more. A girl and a boy. Did you see them?"

Didn't say anything for the longest time. Just kept picking at her dress where there was a hole as big as her hand burned through. I started to turn.

"I had a boy," she said. "I had a son and he went to Antietam and is buried there. I had a son and a store and a husband who ran off and now they're all gone."

"I'm sorry but—"

"I never had slaves. I didn't like slavery. Why did they burn my store?"

"I don't know."

She picked some more, tears cutting the soot on her face, making white streams. "The man you want is Greerson. He owns—I guess owned would be the right way to say it now. He owned the slave yards at the south end of town."

"Thin man, face sharp like an ax, slick hair?"

She nodded. "Yes. He might know what happened to your children. Just go to the south end of town and look for the yards. If you see my husband would you send him home?"

But we were already gone, headed through the broken town, me with my small sack and Lucy with her two hams, looking for the slave yards.

# FOUR

We found the yards and almost got to Greerson in time. Yards were pens with slat-board roofs on them, rings in the wooden walls for chains, chutes that came out to a central open area like there was on the plantation for working with the pigs and cattle.

Same as that. There was some smoke where somebody had tried to fire the pens but the wood wasn't close enough to burn and it went out. The place was empty.

Or almost.

Out front of a small shack was the wagon with the chain rings in it, the wagon that took my children, and I felt the pull of it, felt that it had been close to little Delie and Tyler and thought maybe they were inside the shack but no, nothing there but papers thrown all over, boxes of papers.

"Oh Lord," I said. "They're not here."

There was a sound from the back then. Sound like a hammer hitting meat to soften it ran out around the shack into the main yard opening and there was Greerson.

Not alone though. There was a black man there, big man, hands like my Martin had, shoulders like a door, and he was holding Greerson up against the side fence with one hand and beating him with the other.

Didn't look even mad, the black man. Just as cool were he at a job of work. Hold him with one hand, bring the other back like a club, like a hammer, like a cleaver.

*Chunk!*

In the forehead, in the face, slow hits that seemed to float, but each time Greerson's head snapped back like a mule had kicked him and I forgot for a moment why I was there. Just watched. Then I thought, no, not yet, I need this man.

"Hold!" I said. "Wait. This man took my children and I need him to tell me where they are."

The black man turned and looked at me. "He laid a whip on me. Laid a whip on all of us, but he laid it on me hard. I'm just taking it back. But I can finish later."

He stood to the side but kept holding Greerson up against the fence by the neck. Greerson he just hung there and when I came close I could see that he wasn't going to be doing any talking. His face looked like a wagon had run over it and both his eyes had rolled back to just show white and what breath there was came in little jerks.

"Greerson—can you hear me? You remember coming for my children? Out to the Waller place? You remember that?" But he didn't hear me, didn't hear anything. "You hit him too hard. He ain't there anymore."

"I'm sorry," the black man said, and he looked sorry too. "I didn't know you were coming or I would have held back a tad."

It was Lucy that saved me. I turned away and the black man went back to hitting Greerson and I moved out of the yard and was near crying, thinking of little Delie and Tyler. The wind blew four ways and they could have gone any of them. No way to know.

"In the shack," Lucy said. "There might be something in all those papers about little Delie and Tyler . . ."

And I would have walked away hadn't she said it, would have walked away and never thought of it, never known.

We went inside and started to work. I didn't know what to look for, didn't know where to begin, but Lucy just picked up a piece of paper and went to reading.

"Male, teeth show age not over eighteen, answers to name of Herman, no whip scars, to be at auction. Nope." She threw it aside and picked up another. "Female, teeth show age between twenty-five and thirty, answers to name of Betty, no whip scars, trained for house duties, to be at auction. Nope."

That's what all the papers were. Bills of sale, hundreds and hundreds of them, all records that Greerson kept for all the time he sold slaves.

It was soon dark, too dark to read, but Lucy she found an oil lamp with an unbroken chimney and some matches and soon we had light. Still hard to read but by holding the paper close to the lamp we could make out the letters.

Must have read fifty or a hundred of them when I looked up and Lucy she was sitting there crying, holding the paper.

"What's the matter?"

"I just come across old Willy. You remember him?"

For certain I remembered him. Delie she said that she and old Willy once had eyes for one another. Soft old man used to carve willow whistles for the children in the quarters. Called them whoop-te-do whistles. Gray hair, gray beard, soft voice, soft smile.

"They sold him for fifty dollars," Lucy said. "That was all. Fifty dollars . . ."

And it caught me then, what we were looking at. I had been too much on little Delie and Tyler, couldn't see past my darlings.

Lives. These were lives. All the people we knew and didn't know and Greerson, Waller, all the small evil men had been selling lives. Whole lives. My mammy, pappy, Delie, Billy— didn't matter. All bought and sold, people bought and sold for money, for work, to work to death. Heard once that when they worked the men down in the cane fields south, far south, they figured on the men being dead by twenty and seven. It was the way they worked it out. After they were twenty and seven they started to break and it was easier to just let them die and get newer ones, younger ones.

People. People bought and sold and each of them on these little pieces of paper, each of their lives down to a slip of auction paper. "Answers to name of . . ."

Swore then, swore in my mind so I suppose it's the same as swearing in the open and I hope God he don't get to keeping too close a track on those things. Swore at all the evil that men could do and I cried some with Lucy, cried for the people on the small papers we read in the yellow light from the lamp.

We stopped for a bit and sat, getting sad, but then I shook my head. Crying wouldn't help. "We have to eat something now. So we can keep going."

She took out one of the hams. We didn't have a knife but there was broken glass from the windows and I found a piece and sliced two chunks, thick with fat and smelling of hickory smoke. The smell must have been more than I thought because twice men came to the door while we were eating. One white and the other the same black man who had been beating Greerson. The white man he just looked in and moved on, scared looking, a white face flashing in the lamplight and gone. The black man he came in and we gave him some ham and he chewed it quiet, sitting in the corner, didn't talk to us, never a word and then he left, nodding his thanks for the ham while we went back to the papers.

More lives. We looked all night, paper on paper, and I stacked the ones we read in a neat pile. I couldn't bring myself to throw them away meaning what they meant and just at first gray dawn, sun just starting to help the lamp, Lucy she found it.

"Two children, one boy answers to name of Tyler, girl answers to name of Delie, to be auctioned together or separately—"

I snatched the paper away from her and read but it didn't say more. Just that, to be auctioned. My babies, to be sold. Together or separately? Not that, not apart, not all of us apart. Where were they, when were they sold, who bought them, who bought my babies, my life?

Nothing more on the paper. I turned it over and over but it didn't give nothing. Couldn't think, couldn't do, couldn't make my brain get working again.

"We have to keep looking," Lucy said. "There might be more paper on them." And she picked up another piece, then another, and I nodded and we kept going, kept looking and finally, eyes burning from smoke and no sleep and reading in the dim light all night Lucy she found it again.

"Two young Negro children, answer to Delie and Tyler, sold to William Chivington of New Orleans without auction for three hundred dollars."

I took the paper, hands shaking. Only thing else was the date. One day after they were taken from me. There was no auction. Greerson he must have been worried about what was coming. Wanted to get his money and run, only he didn't run far. Just to his yards. Low man, low as a snake's belly, he laid dead now in the yard where he caused so much misery.

But we had something now. We had a name, the name of the man who bought my children. We had a name and we had a place.

"Where," Lucy asked, "is New Orleans?"

"It's where we're going." Had hope now, had a name, a place. Had hope. Had *something*. "It's where we're going."